*It Always Happens
to Leona*

It Always Happens
to Leona

Juanita Havill
Art by Emily McCully

Crown Publishers, Inc., New York

Published by Crown Publishers, Inc., a Random House company, 225 Park Avenue South,
New York, New York 10003
CROWN is a trademark of Crown Publishers, Inc.
Manufactured in the United States of America

Library of Congress Cataloging-in-Publication Data
Havill, Juanita. It always happens to Leona / Juanita Havill. Summary: Feeling left out
between her older sister and younger brother, Leona decides to run away with Uncle
Rosco, a motorcycle racer. [1. Brothers and sisters—Fiction. 2. Uncles—Fiction.
3. Family life—Fiction.] I. Title.
PZ7.H3115It 1989   [Fic]—dc19   88-39534

ISBN 0-517-57227-3

10 9 8 7 6 5 4 3 2

For the Flanagins,
especially Joan

Contents

1
"Leona, watch what you're doing!"

THE FIRST THING LEONA DID WHEN SHE WOKE UP
was to reach for her lavender straw purse. She opened
the purse to make sure everything was there. In it
were things she would take with her if she ran away:
Band-Aids, toothbrush, a glass monkey, baseball
cards of the entire Chicago White Sox team, and a
piece of her old blanket that Mom had made her
throw away when she finally started school. She had
snitched the monkey from Victoria's collection. But
Victoria had never noticed. She didn't play with her
glass animals anymore.

Leona felt like running away for the first time
when Victoria went to first grade but Leona couldn't.
Then Victoria began to take piano lessons, but Leona
was too young. It was worse after Albert was born.
Her parents didn't have enough time for two children.
Why did they want to have three? And why should
she be the one left out?

Leona climbed down the bunk bed ladder with
her purse and set it on her desk. Then, rubbing sleep
from her eyes, she went downstairs. She heard Daddy's
printer making a racket. Then the printer stopped.
She heard the tapping of his fingers on the computer

keyboard. His office door was closed. Better not bother him.

She stopped at the kitchen doorway. Mom was leaning over, beside Albert's high chair, picking up Cheerios Albert had thrown on the floor. Mom didn't scold him. She never scolded Albert. He could throw the whole carton of milk on the floor and she wouldn't say a word.

"We have a busy day today," Mom said. "I'm going to need your cooperation."

Victoria looked up from the book about African elephants that she was reading while she munched toast. She was wearing her new glasses.

Leona squinted her eyes into tiny slits. She stuck her arms out in front of her and stumbled toward the table.

"Mom, I can't see. I need glasses." Leona bumped the table hard and Albert's orange juice spilled.

"Leona, for heaven's sake. Watch what you're doing," Mom said.

"But I can't see."

"Open your eyes a little. That might help." Mom mopped up the orange juice.

"Leona's just jealous. She wants glasses because I have them," said Victoria.

"No, I don't," said Leona. "I really can't see."

"Leona, the eye doctor said that you have twenty-twenty vision," Mom said. "He told me that you have the eyes of an eagle."

"I do?" said Leona. "I have the eyes of an eagle?" She stuck her tongue out at Victoria. But she couldn't help admiring the round lavender plastic frames that Victoria wore. Victoria looked so important in those glasses. Much more important than anyone who was twelve years old should look.

"Have some cereal, Leona." Mom set the box of cereal in front of Leona.

"I don't like that kind." Leona went to the cupboard to get her favorite cereal, Wrinkle Flakes. No one else in the family would touch them.

"I was telling Victoria and Albert that we have a busy day today," said Mom. "In fact, we have a busy week."

Mom looked around the kitchen, frowning. "I don't know where to start. It's not every day we have a reunion. Your Aunt Gwendolyn, my sister, is coming today. She is taking a whole week off just to visit us and see Uncle Rosco, our little brother. He's coming on Wednesday. He's on his way to drive in a motorcycle race."

"Yippee!" Leona yelled, her mouth full of Wrinkle Flakes. "We're going to a motorcycle race."

"No, Leona. Uncle Rosco is going to a motorcycle race. It's in Tulsa or somewhere. Too far for us to go. He's stopping by on the way."

Leona scooped up a soggy Wrinkle flake with her spoon. "But I want to go to a motorcycle race, too," she said.

"Maybe we can go sometime," Mom said,

"when Uncle Rosco has a race that's closer. Girls, do you remember your aunt and uncle? It's been a long time."

"I remember Aunt Gwendolyn," Victoria said. "She's color coordinated."

"She does dress with style," Mom said. She brushed crumbs off her baggy green sweatshirt with a frown.

"Do I 'member?" Albert asked.

"You were a baby," Leona said. "Babies don't remember."

"I don't know, Albert," said Mom. "You were very little the last time Aunt Gwendolyn and Uncle Rosco came. You were just born."

"I remember Uncle Rosco," said Leona. "He is short and strong. He has curly blond hair and blue eyes, just like me."

"All wrong," said Victoria. "He is tall and skinny and has brown hair and brown eyes like me and Albert. Besides, you were a baby, Leona, and babies can't remember."

"No, I wasn't a baby," said Leona. "I was five years old."

"Don't argue, girls," said Mom. "I need your help. Clean up here when you're finished. After you've dressed, straighten up that room of yours. Swimming lessons this morning and Victoria has to practice piano."

"My side of the room is not messy," said Victoria. "Rita asked me to come over to see her new ten-speed. I'll be back soon. I'll practice after swimming lessons."

Victoria rinsed her bowl, put it in the dishwasher, and ran upstairs to get dressed.

"Me, too," said Leona. "I want to see Rita's bike." She tipped her bowl to her lips and gulped down the last of the Wrinkles and milk. She rushed to set her bowl in the dishwasher. Then she ran up the stairs, tripping twice on her nightgown.

"Leona, your room. Straighten your room first."

"I will, Mom."

It's not fair, Leona thought. Victoria just shoves her things under the bed because she sleeps on the bottom bunk, but I don't have any place to hide my things.

While Victoria put her jeans on, Leona tossed her magnet set, books, crayons, fairy doll, skunk puppet, and clothes onto the top bunk. Then she climbed up and began examining the articles.

"My favorite skirt," she said. "I found my skirt."

"Big deal," said Victoria.

Leona smoothed the wrinkles of her purple-and-green flowered skirt. Perfect to wear to meet Aunt Gwendolyn. Leona dropped the skirt to the floor. She shoved everything else under the covers to the end. There was a big bump like someone sleeping crosswise at the foot of the bed. Leona set her stuffed animals on top of the bump. Then she climbed down and put on her skirt and a ruffled pink blouse.

"I'm ready, Victoria," she shouted, slipping her sandals on.

But Victoria had already gone.

"Wait for me! Wait for me!" Leona shouted. She didn't intend to miss a chance to sit on a ten-speed, even if she hadn't been invited.

2
The Ten-Speed

"LET ME TRY. I WANT TO TRY." LEONA REACHED FOR the handlebars of Rita McIntosh's brand-new ten-speed bicycle.

Rita pushed her bike away from Leona's grasp. "Tell your sister she's too little, Victoria," Rita said.

"You heard Rita," said Victoria. Victoria gripped the handlebars and stepped over the sloping bar. She turned the pedal until it reached the top.

Leona watched Victoria stand up and begin to pedal. Victoria rode the bike along the edge of the street to their driveway half a block away.

Mom was piling beach towels in the back of the station wagon. She stopped and looked when Victoria came along. Albert rushed out of the garage and aimed a stick at Victoria.

"Look, Mom! I can ride Rita's ten-speed!" Victoria yelled.

Leona couldn't hear Mom exactly, but she had a good idea of what she was saying. Something like, "Wonderful. That's great, Victoria." And the next thing she would do would be to go buy Victoria a ten-speed because that's the way it always was. Victoria got everything first: tricycles, bicycles, roller skates, and new clothes. Leona only got hand-me-downs and leftovers that were usually worn out. Then, because Albert was a boy and the "baby," he got everything new—just like Victoria all over again.

Victoria made two more loops in the driveway, then whizzed back to Rita and Leona.

"Mom wants you home now," Victoria said. "Time for swimming lessons. As soon as Aunt Gwendolyn comes, we are leaving."

Victoria stopped the bike. She threw her leg over the bar and stepped to the side with one hand on a handle grip. "A great bike, Rita."

Leona moved in a flash. She grabbed the free handle grip and shoved the bike forward out of Victoria's hand. Before Rita or Victoria could stop her, she stepped on the pedal. She felt the other pedal move around to her foot. Standing, leaning forward, and pedaling hard, she took off down the street.

"Leona, stop right now," Rita ordered.

"Stop, Leona," Victoria shouted and started after Leona.

Leona paid no attention. She felt the wind blow in her face and whistle in her ears. She could feel the bicycle pick up speed as if it had a motor of its own. She couldn't sit on the seat because then her feet wouldn't reach the pedals. Still standing, she gripped the handlebars to keep them steady. She rode over a crack in the sidewalk and wobbled. When she came to the driveway, she had to pedal harder to get over the bump at the bottom.

"Look, Mom. I can ride Rita's ten-speed." Leona

didn't look at Mom because she had to concentrate on the driveway.

"Leona, you're too little for that bike. Be careful," Mom shouted.

"Watch out, Albert," Leona screamed.

Albert jumped in front of Leona. He raised his stick and squinted his eyes. "Pow. Pow. I got you, Leona."

Leona just missed him and the handlebars jerked from side to side. She headed down the driveway and coasted for a moment, picking up speed. Then she squeezed the left-hand brake. Suddenly, Leona and the bike tumbled, right at the edge of the curb.

Leona's right knee throbbed. She looked at it as little beads of blood welled up in a red blotch. Through the handlebars she could see Rita and Victoria running toward her.

"That was dumb," said Victoria.

"Stay off my bike," said Rita. She separated the bike from Leona and righted it. Immediately, she found a bent spoke, and the handlebars were crooked, too.

"Good grief. My bike is brand new," said Rita. "I can't believe you did this to me."

"I'm sorry Rita," Leona said. "Albert got in the way. I can ride it. Did you see me?"

Rita and Victoria stared at Leona in cold silence.

"Come over when you can," Rita said to Victoria. "But please leave her at home. I don't want her to destroy anything else." Rita wheeled her bike up the sidewalk toward her house.

Leona got up slowly and limped after Victoria. Through her tear-bleary eyes she saw Aunt Gwendolyn get out of a car parked in front of their house. Leona hobbled faster.

Aunt Gwendolyn looked like a woman in the Sears catalog. She was wearing a pink blouse and straight gray skirt. She leaned over and gave Victoria a kiss on the head.

"Charming girl," Aunt Gwendolyn said. "And here's your boy. He was just a baby last time. You've grown so tall, Albert," she noted.

Albert raised his stick.

"Don't shoot Aunt Gwendolyn," Leona shouted as she limped toward them.

"Oh my," said Aunt Gwendolyn, looking startled. "You must be Leona." Aunt Gwendolyn patted Leona on the head. Her fingernails were slick and shiny and dark pink.

"I'm the accident-prone one," said Leona, with a sigh.

"Oh," said Aunt Gwendolyn. "I hope not. Mavis, she looks a lot like you."

"Do you think so?" said Mom.

Just then Leona didn't care who she looked like. "I need a Band-Aid on my knee," she said.

Mom examined Leona's knee, and frowned. "Leona, you have to promise to stay off bikes that are not your own. Rita's bike is too big for you. Your legs aren't long enough to reach the pedals."

"But I can ride it. Didn't you see me, Mom?"

"Leona."

"All right. I promise. Can I have a big Band-Aid?"

"I don't want to waste a big Band-Aid. It will just come off at your swimming lesson. Victoria, run in and get the box of Band-Aids, please, and the green bottle and cotton.

"Leona, I wish you would wear jeans when you play. You wouldn't get so scraped up."

"But I like dresses."

Victoria came back with the supplies.

"Ouch." Leona winced when Mom dabbed her knee with liquid from the green bottle. "That hurts."

"Be brave, Leona," said Aunt Gwendolyn.

"I am brave," said Leona. "But I wish my legs were longer."

3
High Dive

"DIVE, LEONA," THE SWIMMING TEACHER SAID.

This was Leona's reward for doing such a good job swimming. She was the fastest swimmer in her Advanced Beginners class at the High School Pool. Leona was sure she should be in Intermediates with Victoria. She could hold her breath for a long time. She could swim the crawl on her belly and back. She could swim halfway across the pool with her eyes open (Victoria always closed her eyes), and she could run and jump off the diving board feet first.

But it wasn't so easy to get her head to go in the water first. Her head didn't want to go first.

"Just bend over, tuck your chin, and fall in," the instructor said.

Leona was afraid her tummy was too round for her to stay bent over. She put her hands together, leaned forward, and aimed toward the water. Then she wondered if Mom was watching. With her hands still above her head, she looked up at the bleachers and saw Mom talking to Aunt Gwendolyn.

Aunt Gwendolyn pointed to the high diving board. It was at the opposite end of the pool, straight across from Leona. Victoria was standing on the end of it.

Leona's hands dropped to her sides. She watched Victoria lean over and fall straight into the pool, with her arms outstretched and her toes pointed.

Mom and Aunt Gwendolyn clapped.

"The first time on the high board and she dived right off," said Mom.

"If you are not going to dive, Leona, please jump," said her instructor. "Others are waiting."

"Okay," Leona said. She waved to her mom. "Look, Mom. Look, Aunt Gwendolyn. Watch me dive."

She gulped a mouthful of air and bent over. I've got to do it, she told herself. Head first. She felt as if her toes were glued to the board. Then she closed her eyes, leaned forward, and fell—*ker-splat*—belly first on the surface of the pool. Leona coughed and sputtered for a moment. The whole front of her body hurt as if she had been stung by a thousand bees, from her chin to her knees. She rolled over onto her back and kicked to the ladder.

"Keep your chin down, Leona. You'll have it soon," the instructor said.

"Not bad," Aunt Gwendolyn said from the bleachers.

"Be careful, Leona," said Mom.

Leona picked up her towel and wrapped it around herself. She felt shivery and cold and somehow smaller than she had a minute ago.

Albert was almost through with his lesson. He lined up at the board with a dozen three-year-olds. Their instructor treaded water beneath the board and coaxed them to jump. They all wore fat, orange life jackets and the first few would not jump. But Albert toddled right off the end of the board and landed like a happy duck in front of the teacher.

Mom and Aunt Gwendolyn both clapped and shouted, "Good job, Albert."

Albert climbed up the ladder and said, "I jump good. Watch me jump again," and tromped onto the board.

Show-off, Leona thought. She looked at the high board. No one was there. Victoria and her class were stacking their kickboards at the other end of the pool. Leona let her towel drop from her shoulders and moved toward the board.

Up the red metal ladder she climbed, slowly, because the steps were far between. She looked down through the space between the steps to see how far she had climbed.

"Lesson's over. Everybody out." The swimming instructors blew their whistles all at once.

Leona felt a tremble in her tummy. She didn't look back. She pretended not to hear. She was up too high now. She stepped onto the board and gripped the metal side rails. She walked to the end.

"You shouldn't be up there," Victoria shouted from across the pool.

"Climb back down," Victoria's instructor said. She hurried to the high board. "You don't have to jump if you're afraid to."

Leona looked down. The water was deep and clear. She could see the thick tar strips all the way down on the pale blue bottom. She pulled off the

Band-Aid that hung from her knee and dropped it in the water. It took forever to fall. It finally landed and began to sink. What a jump! Leona hesitated. She felt like everyone was staring at her—silently.

Just to be sure, she shouted, "Look, Mom, Aunt Gwendolyn."

She took a deep breath, pinched her nose, and leaped.

For about two seconds it was wonderful. Leona was flying, like a bird, like a sky diver, straight to the water. Then it was over. She went so far under the water that she almost ran out of breath before she got to the top. Her elbow smarted where it had smacked against the water's surface.

Leona paddled to the ladder, panting. She climbed out. Victoria was waiting for her.

"You're in trouble, Leona," Victoria said, and handed her a towel.

"Don't ever go off the high dive without your instructor's permission," Victoria's teacher said.

Leona's teacher ran up. "Leona, I won't even let you jump off the low board if you do something like that again."

"I'm sorry," said Leona. But she wasn't sorry. She didn't feel bad or ashamed. She was sure that Mom had seen her go off the high board, and Aunt Gwendolyn, too. Maybe next time she would dive.

The water in the shower was warm. It dribbled down in a soft spray on Leona's face and shoulders and took the sting away. Her scraped knee even felt better.

She shampooed her hair three times just to stay in the shower. Then she rubbed on gobs of conditioner. It was creamy and smelled good enough to eat. She touched her tongue to a glob on her hand. "Yuck," she said, spitting it out. Maybe if she used enough conditioner, it would straighten her curls. She would have slick, shiny hair like Victoria. That's what her hair felt like in the shower, shiny and slick and straight.

Leona turned the shower off. She was the only one left. She rubbed her hair in a hurry and got dressed. When she ran out into the hall, no one was there.

"Mom! Victoria! Albert! Aunt Gwendolyn!" she cried as she ran toward the door. Why had they left her? How could they forget about her, Leona Joan Hanrahan, who had just jumped for the very first time off the high dive?

Leona pushed the door. It wouldn't budge. It must have been locked. From the inside? Where did everybody go? Leona pushed on the other door. It was locked, too.

"Mo-om! He-elp!" she shouted. She pounded on the glass door, but no one came.

Leona couldn't believe they were doing this to her. Mom, Victoria, Albert, and Aunt Gwendolyn had piled into the car and driven back home. They would all sit down and have lunch without her. They wouldn't even miss her. Swimming lessons ended at noon. Leona would have to sit in the hall until the pool opened at two in the afternoon.

"Looks like you're locked in," said a voice behind her. "I heard you calling."

It was the janitor. He pressed a small button on the door handle. "You must be real late to get yourself locked in here."

He pushed the door open and held it for Leona.

"Gosh. I'm glad you came. My family just forgot about me." Leona rushed through.

"How could they forget about someone like you?" the janitor called after her.

Leona ran out to the parking lot. Mom sat in the front seat drumming her fingers on the steering wheel.

Victoria opened the side door.

"Leona, I don't have to tell you how tired we all are of waiting for you," Mom said. "You know how busy we are today. You should have hurried. Think of Aunt Gwendolyn, who came to lessons with us instead of resting a bit after her long trip."

"I'm sorry, Mom. But the door was locked."

"It's no wonder. You took so long," Mom said.

"Mom, did you see me jump off the high dive?"

"Yes, I did, Leona. And I also saw the teacher scold you. Leona, you should try to be more responsible."

"But Mom," said Leona. Then she settled against the back seat and stared out the window. Responsible. What did being responsible have to do with jumping off the high dive?

4
All Gone

WHEN THEY GOT BACK HOME FROM THE POOL, everyone was thirsty. They all went to the kitchen to have a drink of fruit juice.

"Victoria, you can practice before lunch," Mom said. "Gwendolyn, maybe you would like to change into something more comfortable."

"I'm fine," said Aunt Gwendolyn. "Let me help with lunch."

"Relax," said Mom. "I have everything under control."

"Can I have a peanut-butter-and-banana sandwich for lunch?" Leona said.

"No, not today. We are having pocket bread filled with marinated vegetables."

"Yuck," said Leona. "Why can't we have peanut butter?"

"Mavis, you don't feed your children too much peanut better, do you?" Aunt Gwendolyn asked Mom.

"I try not to," Mom said.

"I have to eat peanut butter every day," said Leona. Leona started to tell Aunt Gwendolyn all of the different ways to eat peanut butter, but Mom interrupted.

"Leona, please take Albert to the bathroom."

"Do I have to?" Leona said. The look on Mom's face said "Yes."

"Come on, Albert."

"I don't have to go."

"You do, too," Leona said. "Mom said so."

"No, I don't." Albert stuck his lower lip out and squinted.

"Yes, you do."

"No, I don't."

"I think I'll listen to Victoria practice," Aunt Gwendolyn said, hurrying from the kitchen.

Mom frowned. "Try to cooperate, Leona."

"Tell Albert to cooperate."

"I will, but honestly, Leona, you have only been making things worse today. First, Rita's bicycle. Then the diving board. Couldn't you try to be more grown-up? Aunt Gwendolyn doesn't have children. She's not used to all the confusion. And she's tired after driving for two days. Please take Albert to the bathroom. Albert, go with Leona."

Leona shrugged. "Let's go, Albert."

"If you read me the soldier story." Albert ran to get his book from a shelf in the fireplace room. Then he carried his book to the bathroom at the end of the hall.

Leona followed him.

"Drummer Hoff fires it off," Albert sang and pulled his shorts down.

"Albert, you did too have to go." Leona pointed

to his messy underwear. She groaned and pinched her nose. "I'm going to get Mom."

"I don't want Mom," Albert said. He looked worried. "I want you, Leona."

"Oh ugh, Albert. I'm too young to clean up after babies. No wonder Aunt Gwendolyn doesn't have a baby. They're too messy."

"I'm not a baby. Please, Leona, help me." Albert's brown eyes filled to the brim with tears. He looked so sad and cute even if he didn't smell so good. Albert stepped out of his shorts and underwear.

"Oh, all right." Still pinching her nose, Leona grasped the underwear with her thumb and forefinger. She dropped it in the toilet bowl, as she had seen Mom do. "This will have to soak.

"Now let's take care of you, Albert. You sit in the bathtub. I'll get you something else to wear."

Leona ran the water into the tub while Albert climbed in.

"It's too cold, Leona."

"Daddy says cold water is good for you." Leona turned the water off. "It makes you strong and healthy."

"You mean it gives me strong muscles?"

"Very strong muscles. Now sit down."

"But I want strong muscles in my arms."

"Splash water on them," Leona said.

Albert began to splash water on his arms. Leona slipped out of the bathroom and went upstairs to get Albert clean underwear.

While she was there, Leona also rescued her lavender purse. Albert had set it in the middle of the floor and surrounded it with soldiers. Leona put her purse back in her room, on top of her bed.

She decided Albert needed to stay in the bath a little longer. She wanted to peek in the guest room. She opened the door a crack and saw Aunt Gwendolyn's burgundy suitcase on the couch. The suitcase was open. She could see silky yellow material on top. Was it a nightgown or a fancy party dress? Leona stepped into the guest room to see.

The yellow material was a nightgown. Underneath the nightgown were yellow satin slippers and underneath the slippers were two blue velvet bags with sandals in them. Then came the bottom of the suitcase.

Leona looked up and saw a gold bag on the dressing table. It was unzipped. She pushed the sides of the bag apart and stared at the tubes and bottles and brushes in the bag.

"Makeup. Wow! I never saw so much lipstick," Leona said to herself.

Mom never had makeup around. Mom said, "I quit wearing makeup when I quit my job at the bank. It doesn't hurt to pinch pennies. Makeup is so expensive."

The contents of Aunt Gwendolyn's bag must have cost thousands of dollars. Maybe that was why she was so beautiful. All of that makeup probably made people notice Aunt Gwendolyn.

5

It Always Happens to Leona

THE PLUMBER COULDN'T COME UNTIL TOMORROW
to fix the downstairs toilet.

Aunt Gwendolyn kept saying, "I'm so sorry,"
and then Mom said, "It was just an accident."

But when Leona said she was sorry, Mom said,
"Why couldn't you be more careful?"

Albert didn't seem bothered at all. If it was
anybody's fault in the first place, it was Albert's.

After lunch, Leona made a sign that said OUT
OF ORDER and taped it to the toilet seat. Then she
went up to her room and sat on her bed. She held her
purse and felt sorry for a long time. Her purse made
her feel better. It was a friend who had the answer to
all her problems. The lavender purse made her think
better, too. It made her think, If these people don't
like you, find someone who does. Run away. And
they'll be sorry.

Leona lay down on the lump at the end of her
bed. The trouble was, if she ran away now, she
wouldn't see Uncle Rosco. Leona didn't want to miss
Uncle Rosco. She stared at the ceiling and tried to
imagine what her mom's brother would be like. Then
she fell asleep.

"Leona, Leona, come help me," Mom called.

Leona woke. She grabbed the guard rail and dropped to the floor like a monkey. She ran downstairs.

"Oh, Leona, there you are. Where have you been? I called you earlier."

"I was in my room."

"I wanted you to help me whip the cream, but you are too late now."

"I didn't hear you, Mom. Can I help you lick the beaters?"

"I've already washed them. But you can put the napkins 'round." Mom handed her the linen napkins. "And you can tell Daddy it's time for dinner."

Leona carried the napkins into the dining room. She loved the dark-blue napkins with swirls of dainty white lace stitched to the edges. She set a napkin beside each plate and then ran down the hall to Daddy's office.

She knocked three times, as loud as she could. Then she opened the door and rushed in. "Time for supper. We're eating on fancy plates with fancy napkins."

"We'll be right there."

Daddy and Albert were standing in front of the computer screen, staring at the image of a chubby robot that Daddy had programmed. The robot began to sing, "Daisy, Daisy." Albert jumped up and down. When the song ended, Albert clapped and said, "Do it again."

"Daddy, can you make the horse that jumps?"
Leona asked. "I haven't seen the horse in a long time."

"Not now," Daddy said. "You said it yourself.
It's time to eat."

"Then after supper," Leona said, "please."

"We'll see." Daddy switched off the computer.
"Come on, Albert. Let's wash our hands. You, too,
Leona."

"I don't have to," Albert said.

Daddy led him out of the office and turned the
light off, leaving Leona in the dark.

"Thanks a lot," Leona said.

Roast lamb, baked potatoes, carrots cooked with
mushrooms and onions. A grown-up meal, for sure.
Why couldn't Aunt Gwendolyn like peanut butter instead? Leona noticed a thick white glob on her
Jell-O salad. She grabbed her spoon while Victoria
said the prayer, "We thank thee, O Lord, for these
thy gifts . . ." Leona mouthed the words and finished
first. She scooped the cream off the Jello-O and into
her mouth.

"*Blech!*" she shouted just as everyone said, "A-
men."

"Leona, what is the matter with you?" Mom
said.

"This isn't whipped cream, Mom," Leona said.
"Where is the whipped cream?"

"It's mayonnaise," said Mom. "The whipped
cream is for dessert, which you will not have if you
don't straighten up."

Mom's face was red. She pushed her hair off her

forehead and Leona could see it was wet. Mom was hot and tired from cooking. That's why she was grumpy.

"Your mother's right," Daddy said. "Make an effort, Leona. I heard that you have not had a very good day."

"You mustn't blame her for the plumbing problem," Aunt Gwendolyn said. "That was an unfortunate accident. It could have happened to anyone."

"But it happened to Leona," Victoria said. She rolled her eyes upward and shrugged. "It always does."

Leona glared at Victoria. Victoria smiled back. Victoria's lips were very pink. Her cheeks were, too. She didn't look hot and sweaty like Mom. Leona put a slice of carrot in her mouth and stared some more. Victoria's face seemed to sparkle. Above her eyes was a dusting of silver frost.

Makeup, Leona thought. She started to shout, but the carrot slipped down her throat before she had time to chew it. It was a big piece and it ached all the way down. Leona gulped water from her glass and blinked back the tears that formed in her eyes. She was going to ask Aunt Gwendolyn to let her try the makeup. But no, as usual, Victoria had been first. But if Leona told and got Victoria in trouble right now, she might never get to try Aunt Gwendolyn's makeup.

Aunt Gwendolyn looked at Victoria. They smiled at each other the way Victoria and Rita did when they were keeping a secret from Leona. This time, Leona knew what the secret was.

"Leona, do you have to go to the bathroom?"
Mom said.

"No."

"Then don't squirm at the table."

It was hard not to wiggle when she could see
Victoria's silver eye shadow, pink lips, and frosted
fingernails. She wanted to shout in her loudest voice,
"Victoria's wearing makeup!"

"Leona, go to the bathroom," Daddy said.

"But I don't have to."

"Leona, don't argue," Daddy said in his serious
voice. "And you have to use the upstairs bathroom."

This is crazy, Leona thought. Victoria is sitting
at the table covered with makeup and I'm the one
who has to go upstairs.

She stomped up the stairs. She knew, if she
turned around, Mom and Daddy would be frowning
at her.

Leona went into the bathroom and got a drink
of water. She looked in the mirror at her pale face and
her tangled hair. If Victoria can, so can I, she thought,
and tiptoed into the guest room.

The gold bag was open on the dressing table.
Tubes and bottles and brushes lay beside it. Leona sat
down and pulled the shiny tops off the tubes to see
all the colors. Red, brown, purple, pink, and green.
A color to go with every outfit. Aunt Gwendolyn had
so much lipstick that she would never know if Leona
used any.

Leona chose brown to match her sandals. She

rubbed a brown circle onto her lips. She pressed her lips together and smiled at herself in the mirror. Not bad.

Leona looked at her green skirt. Then she smeared the green makeup over her eyes. She found a compact of purple, sparkly powder and patted it all over her face. When she looked at the face in the mirror, she wondered why she didn't look like Aunt Gwendolyn. She didn't look like Leona, either.

In one tube, Leona found a tiny black brush. For the eyelashes, she thought, and tried to paint her pale lashes black. Instead, she poked her eye. That hurt, so she rubbed. Black smeared around her eye and tears oozed out. Back went the mascara brush.

Leona sprayed perfume on her neck. Then she chose brown nail polish to match her lips.

It was hard to paint her nails. Her hands kept shaking. Aunt Gwendolyn must have done Victoria's nails for her. When Leona touched her thumb to see if it was dry, she smudged a dent in the slick, shiny surface.

"Leona, hurry up," Victoria called from the bottom of the stairs. "It's time for dessert."

Leona jumped and dropped the nail brush. It painted a thin brown streak on the pink blouse hanging on the chair behind her. She grabbed the brush, stuck it back in the bottle, and ran out of the room. She stopped at the top of the stairs and took a deep breath. She could feel her heart beating as fast as if she had just run around the block.

6
Aunt Gwendolyn

WHEN LEONA WAS HALFWAY DOWN THE STAIRS, SHE heard "oohs" and "ahs" coming from the dining room.

Dessert!

Leona bounded down the stairs, forgetting to be elegant or grown-up.

"Save some for me," she said, plopping into her chair.

"I did," said Mom. "You can have it as soon as you finish your supper." She set a dessert plate beside Leona's water glass. The plate was filled with short-cake, strawberries, and a mound of whipped cream.

Mom looked at Leona and her mouth dropped open. Victoria gasped. Daddy stared. Aunt Gwendolyn arched her left eyebrow. Leona looked down at her plate and tried to concentrate on the cold roast lamb. It's not polite to stare, she thought.

"Leona is a clown," Albert said and pointed at her. "A clown. A clown."

"I am not," Leona said.

"All right, Leona," Mom said, "tell me where you got that makeup. You know you are not supposed to wear makeup."

"I know," said Leona. "Victoria isn't supposed

to wear makeup, either." Leona hadn't meant to say that, but it came out anyway.

Mom looked at Victoria. So did Daddy.

"Victoria, is it true?" Mom said. "Are you wearing makeup?"

"Yes," said Victoria. She stared at Leona as if she wanted to pinch her.

"Mavis," Aunt Gwendolyn said, "I didn't know you were strict about makeup. Victoria is twelve and I just put a little on her, very lightly. She has such lovely eyes."

"Her eyes look just as lovely without eye shadow."

"It doesn't hurt to help nature," Aunt Gwendolyn said.

Mom frowned.

"Let's not make a fuss," Daddy said. "Why don't you girls just clean up and that will be that."

"I'll help them." Aunt Gwendolyn stood up.

Leona jumped up.

"Wait, Leona," Mom said. "I want to ask you something. You don't look like Aunt Gwendolyn made you up, too. Where did you get your makeup?"

"I borrowed it." Leona tried not to look at Aunt Gwendolyn. She hoped that Aunt Gwendolyn would begin to understand. She wanted to hear her say, "Well, Leona is eight years old and she has such beautiful eyes."

Aunt Gwendolyn didn't say anything.

"You didn't ask, did you?" Mom said.

"I didn't have time. If there was time, Aunt Gwendolyn would have done my eyes, too." Leona turned to Aunt Gwendolyn.

"You are a little young, Leona," Aunt Gwendolyn said. "But I'll show you how to take it off the right way."

"Tell Aunt Gwendolyn you're sorry, Leona."

"I'm sorry," said Leona.

"All right," said Aunt Gwendolyn. "Come on now."

Aunt Gwendolyn and Victoria and Leona headed for the stairs.

"After you are clean, Leona, could you get ready for bed? It is getting late. I'll save your shortcake for you for tomorrow," Mom said.

Leona groaned. But she didn't complain out loud. At least she got to go and learn how to take off makeup.

Aunt Gwendolyn showed Victoria and Leona how to use cotton balls and makeup remover. Victoria was very skillful. She finished quickly. Leona heard Aunt Gwendolyn whisper, "Do you mind if I help Leona alone?" Victoria smiled smugly and went back downstairs.

"There. Doesn't that look better?" Aunt Gwendolyn said to Leona.

Leona stared at her face in the mirror. She looked at her lips and her eyes. The green was gone. Her cheeks were white again. Her eyelashes were still wet and stuck together.

"I don't know," said Leona.

"Of course you do. You look like a nice little girl."

"A pale little girl that no one ever notices."

"I don't know, Leona. You're pretty hard to miss. Who is it that doesn't notice you?"

"Mom and Daddy. Haven't you seen how Victoria and Albert get all the attention around here?"

"I just got here this morning." Aunt Gwendolyn picked up the hairbrush and ran it through Leona's hair. The brush made a bristly, rustling noise.

"Ouch," said Leona.

"But what did you do to your hair? It's so sticky," said Aunt Gwendolyn.

"Conditioner. I put on a lot to make my hair straight and shiny."

"It didn't really work, did it?" Aunt Gwendolyn said. "You have to rinse conditioner out." Aunt Gwendolyn pulled the brush through Leona's curls. "This might hurt a bit."

Leona blinked hard. Her head hurt all over. She looked at Aunt Gwendolyn's face in the mirror. Aunt Gwendolyn had dark eyebrows that curved like a movie star's. She had thick eyelashes and brown eyes.

"You don't understand, Aunt Gwendolyn. You're beautiful. Everyone probably notices you."

"I won't make up a story to tell you how plain

and shy I was." Aunt Gwendolyn frowned as she tried to fluff Leona's hair. "Because that's not the truth. But I was the oldest child in the family. I had to be responsible. I tried hard to do my best and to be good, too."

"But you didn't have to try to be beautiful," Leona said.

"That takes a lot of work, too." Aunt Gwendolyn shook her hair over her shoulders. "I wish your mother made more of an effort."

"Mom says you have it or you don't. Why waste time? She says actions speak louder than looks."

"Now that's something to think about, Leona. What you do."

"But I try to do the right thing. It just doesn't always work."

"Maybe you have to try harder. You have to make up your mind, no matter what, to be good and helpful."

Aunt Gwendolyn sounded like her swimming teacher. "You have to make up your mind to dive, Leona." Leona knew she could learn to dive. It wasn't that hard. She could probably be good, too, if she made up her mind to.

"All right," Leona said. "From now on I am going to be so good you won't know me."

Aunt Gwendolyn got a hanger from the closet and lifted her silk blouse from the back of the chair.

Leona gasped.

"What's wrong?" Aunt Gwendolyn asked. Then she saw the long brown drip of nail polish on her blouse.

Aunt Gwendolyn's eyes went cold. Leona could see her face become a mask. Aunt Gwendolyn ran her finger down the streak of lacquer.

"It was an accident," Leona said. "I'm sorry. I won't ever do it again. It could have happened to anybody."

"But it happened to you," said Aunt Gwendolyn. "I mean it happened to me, to my silk blouse. Why did you have to do it?"

Aunt Gwendolyn didn't have any kids, but she was beginning to sound like a mom. Leona waited for her to say "I'm exasperated with you, Leona. Go to your room."

Instead, Aunt Gwendolyn's voice sounded far away. "I'm sure I can have this blouse cleaned somehow. We won't even tell your mother. But please don't use my makeup again."

"Aunt Gwendolyn, I will never open your nail polish bottle again." Leona was surprised at how easy it was to say that. She hoped it would be just as easy to stay out of trouble.

The rest of the evening went smoothly. Dad took Albert upstairs to read him a story and put him to bed. Leona sat on the sofa with Victoria and Mom and Aunt Gwendolyn, and looked at the family photo album Aunt Gwendolyn had brought.

Aunt Gwendolyn was beautiful even when she was a kid. Leona couldn't believe that the little chubby girl in cowboy boots was Mom. It was hard to tell what Uncle Rosco looked like. He made faces. Aunt Gwendolyn said he ruined every picture he was in.

When they went to bed, Victoria told Leona that Aunt Gwendolyn had invited her, just her all alone, to visit sometime.

"So what," Leona said. Victoria had just said that to get even because Leona told about the makeup.

"Aunt Gwendolyn is very important," Victoria went on. "She works in public relations and buys all her own clothes. She's not like Mom."

"Mom used to work," Leona said. "She worked at a bank once. When Albert was born, she painted rock jewelry."

"Painting rocks is not where it's at."

"Where what's at?"

"Where you can be somebody."

"Mom's somebody," Leona said.

"Somebody grouchy."

Leona climbed up the ladder and pulled the cover up. She set her purse by her pillow.

"Aunt Gwendolyn can be grouchy, too." Leona thought about the silk blouse and Aunt Gwendolyn's cold stare. There are different kinds of grouchy.

7
The Purse Snatcher

LEONA LEANED OVER THE EDGE OF THE TOP BUNK. Victoria was already up. It must be late. She reached under her pillow for her purse, but it wasn't there. Maybe it had fallen on the floor. Leona climbed down to look. Her purse wasn't on the floor or under the bed or on her desk, either.

She was pretty sure she had taken it to bed with her, but last night was so mixed up, maybe she left it downstairs. She would look after she got dressed.

Leona put on her pink jumper and her white blouse. Then she ran down to breakfast. No one was there. She looked out the back door and saw the plumber drive away in his little white van. Albert was picking raspberries with Mom in the backyard.

An empty bowl and a glass of orange juice sat at her place at the table. The orange juice was as warm as bath water. Leona poured it in the sink and suddenly remembered the strawberry shortcake. Mom had said she could have it today.

Leona had almost finished the most delicious breakfast she had ever had in her life when Mom came in the back door with a bucket full of raspberries.

"Good morning, Mom," said Leona.

"Why, Leona, you're already dressed. You look nice."

Leona licked whipped cream off her upper lip and forked a whole strawberry into her mouth.

"But you shouldn't be eating dessert for breakfast."

"You said I could eat it today."

"I didn't mean for breakfast."

"Strawberry shortcake is a good breakfast. Strawberries for fruit group. Whipped cream for milk and cake for cereal."

"That's one way to look at it. You are pretty sharp this morning, aren't you?"

Leona smiled. "Where's Aunt Gwendolyn?" she whispered. "Is she still asleep?"

"Oh no. She took Victoria shopping."

"Shopping! Why didn't you wake me up? Why would I want to sleep when I could go shopping?"

"You were so tired after yesterday," Mom said. "Anyway, Aunt Gwendolyn is going to buy outfits for both of you."

"But I have to try it on."

"I told her your size," Mom said.

"But she doesn't know my style," said Leona.

"I think you can trust Aunt Gwendolyn's judgment."

"She should buy you an outfit, too, Mom," Leona said.

"Thanks." Mom rolled up the sleeves of her baggy sweatshirt.

Leona thought about the pictures that Aunt Gwendolyn showed them last night. "Mom, did you really wear cowboy boots?"

"They were my favorite," Mom said. "I had pearl

buttons on my jeans and cowboy shirt. Most of the
girls wore dresses. Gwendolyn did, for sure."

"Mom, did you ever feel left out?" Leona said.

Mom put her arm around Leona's shoulder.
Leona felt good all over. She leaned against Mom and
waited for her to squeeze and give her a kiss or ruffle
her hair. She closed her eyes and listened for Mom to
say, "I always felt left out, because my mom and dad
never paid any attention to me."

Instead, Leona heard Albert bang the screen door
open. "Mom. Mom. Soldier flew. Help me get my soldier."

Mom let go of Leona's shoulder. "Never a dull
moment," she said and hurried out the back door.

"I wish Albert would fly away with his soldiers,"
Leona said. Albert was always throwing his soldiers
in the air to make them fly. One of them probably
got stuck on a branch and Mom had to shake it down.

Leona wondered if Aunt Gwendolyn was right
about being good. Did it really make others notice
you? Mom had noticed her jumper this morning. But
Mom had noticed Albert, too. Right away. And Albert hadn't been good at all.

Leona shook her head. I guess I should try anyway, she thought. She started by rinsing her bowl
and putting it in the dishwasher.

Mom came back into the kitchen. Leona was
going to ask her what she could do to help. Then she
saw Albert.

"Albert, what are you doing with my purse?"
she shouted.

8
Rescue Attempt

ALBERT WAS DRAGGING THE LAVENDER PURSE across the floor by one handle. The purse was open and baseball cards trailed across the floor. Leona could see a tangle of plastic soldiers in the purse.

"A house for my soldiers," said Albert.

"That's my purse. You took it. Now give it back." Leona grabbed one handle of the purse.

"No." Albert tugged the other handle.

Leona pulled harder. She was so mad she wanted to pinch Albert and make him let go. Then she remembered that she had decided to be good and help Mom. Was this any way to help Mom? No, she thought, and let go of the purse handle.

Albert sat down with a *bam*.

"Owie, owie," he said and began to cry. "You pushed me. Leona pushed me, Mom."

"No, I didn't, Albert. You fell. Besides, I am not going to fight over my purse."

"Not fight?"

"No," said Leona. She took her baseball cards and other supplies from the purse and set them on the kitchen counter—as far back as she could reach. Then she closed it and fastened it shut. "But you'd better be careful with it."

Albert took the purse and held it to his chest in a bear hug.

"That's nice of you, Leona," said Mom. "I was just going to ask you to help me out. Could you play with Albert in the backyard while I fix lunch?"

Play with Albert? Leona groaned. Hadn't yesterday been enough? "Couldn't I help you make lunch?"

"I really need you to watch Albert and to keep him out of the kitchen."

Mom needs me, Leona thought. But why did being helpful mean having to do things she didn't like to do? "Oh, all right. Come on, Albert."

Albert clung to the purse and rushed outside.

Leona had expected Albert to lose interest in her purse and drop it. She had to muster every ounce of goodness to keep from knocking him down and getting her purse back. She followed Albert across the patio to the backyard.

"Want to swing, Albert?"

"No."

"Come on, Albert. I'll push."

"No," said Albert.

He stopped at the sandbox, which was at the edge of the patio.

"Don't put my purse in the sand," Leona scolded.

Albert set the purse down very carefully beside the sandbox. Then he pushed it along the wooden rim. "*Vrrrm. Rrrr.* Let's go, soldiers."

Leona winced as she sat in the swing. "Okay,

Albert, have it your way. Mom will make you give me my purse back later."

"No," said Albert.

"You'll see," said Leona. "Mom will make you."

Thinking about her purse made her mad. Leona decided to swing and not think about Albert anymore. She leaned back and then forward and pumped and flew straight over the backyard. Then she flew back again. Leona stretched her legs until they touched the sky. She whizzed back and forth. The swing creaked. The sun felt warm. I can fly like a bird, she thought.

At the very highest point, Leona let go of the swing and straightened her body. She arched into the air—fly, fly, fly—and landed feet first on the grass. Then she lost her balance and sat down hard. *Oof.* Her feet tingled and her bottom hurt.

"Albert," Leona said, getting up, "are you sure you don't want to swing?"

Albert ran to the swing and climbed in.

"Where's my purse?" Leona looked at the sandbox. A platoon of plastic soldiers perched on the rim. The purse wasn't there. She turned around and scanned the yard. No lavender purse.

"Albert, what did you do with my purse?"

"Push me, Leona," Albert said.

"I'll push you when you tell me what you did with my purse."

Albert smiled. "The purse flew high. Like a jet."

"And where did it land?"

Albert pointed toward the house. There on the

roof of the fireplace room sat the lavender purse. It was more than an arm's reach from the roof edge.

"Albert, are you ever in trouble. How did you do that?"

Albert beamed. "It flew," he said.

I will not get mad, Leona told herself. The last thing Leona wanted to do was bother Mom. Mom had asked for her help and Leona didn't want to mess up now. But it was really hard to be good around Albert. If Leona were Albert's mom, she would make him go to his room for a whole week. And he couldn't have anything to eat but boiled cabbage and prunes.

"I'll have to do it by myself," Leona said. "Albert, bad boy. Go sit in the sandbox."

"No," said Albert.

"Albert, don't you ever feel a tiny bit sorry?"

"No."

Leona had a very bad thought of wanting to make Albert feel sorry. Being good was getting harder and harder.

"Then stay out of my way," she said to Albert.

Leona found the window-washing ladder leaning lengthwise against the fireplace room. Daddy always said it was as light as a fly, but when Leona lugged the ladder and set it beneath the overhanging roof, she thought he must be talking about the heaviest fly in the universe.

She remembered how Victoria had climbed up the ladder last week to help Daddy fix a leak in the roof by the chimney. No big deal, she thought. If Victoria can, so can I.

Leona climbed to the next to the last step. Not high enough. She stood on top of the ladder. Still she couldn't reach the purse. Slowly she climbed up onto the overhanging roof, rubbing her scraped knee.

"Ouch," she said loudly. But it was worth the pain in her knee. She reached for her purse handle and pulled it to her. Then she turned around to see where to put her foot on the ladder. But the ladder was leaning to the side at an odd angle. Suddenly, it crashed across the sandbox.

"Albert," Leona murmured.

Mom came running out the back door. "What on earth was that?" she said.

"The ladder fell," said Albert.

"Are you all right, Albert? You shouldn't be playing with the ladder. Where's Leona? She is supposed to be watching you."

The last thing Leona wanted was for Mom to look up and see her sitting on the roof. That didn't fit her new image at all. That was something the old Leona would have done to be noticed—climb on the roof and sit there.

Mom didn't look up. Leona sighed.

"Leona went up," Albert said.

"I wish she would be more responsible," said Mom. She took Albert's hand. "Let's go inside now."

Albert looked up at Leona. He didn't say a word. He didn't smile or frown or shout or point. But even from her perch on the roof, Leona could see something sparkle in his dark-brown eyes.

9
The View from Above

LEONA SAT ON THE SCRATCHY ROOF SHINGLES, IN the hot sun. Being on the roof was a kind of punishment. It was worse than going to her room. She wished she could be in her room right now.

Mom would never understand about the roof. She would probably yell at her. Daddy would be mad, too, if he found out. Definitely, Aunt Gwendolyn would think Leona had failed at trying to be good.

If no one came out the back door, she could climb down without being noticed. It would be the first time in her whole life that she didn't want to be noticed. If she could get down, no one would know she had been stuck on the roof. No one except Albert, and he wasn't talking. If he did tell about flying jet-plane purses, everyone would just think it was a cute story.

But the ladder was on the ground. There wasn't a sturdy branch in sight. If only Leona had a telephone, she could call Rita and ask her to come and put the ladder back up and not tell anyone. Except Rita would never help her now, not after she had wrecked Rita's bike. It was no use to call Teddy or Madge. They were on vacation. She could call the fire department. But if the fire department came, Mom would notice. Anyway, she didn't have a phone.

Maybe she could jump. Leona looked over the edge of the roof. It wasn't even as high as the high board. But Leona knew that the brick walk below was a lot harder than the water at the pool. She knew all about how hard the ground is when you jump out of swings or down from trees. Leona had a lot of experience.

The back door swung open.

"I'm not going to wait any longer. Leona will just have to eat later." Mom carried a tray of sandwiches to the round table in the middle of the patio.

Aunt Gwendolyn followed with a big salad bowl.

"Victoria, bring some cups and the pitcher of lemonade on the counter," Mom shouted, "and tell Daddy lunch is ready."

"Albert has quite an imagination," Aunt Gwendolyn said. She put the salad bowl down on the patio table. "As soon as we got home, he ran out to tell about a flying purple purse." Aunt Gwendolyn laughed.

"Well," said Mom, "he must have imagined that Leona was in her room, too. She certainly isn't. She's probably at the neighbors', but she knows we have company. She should be home for lunch."

Leona pulled her knees to her chest and hunched her shoulders. She knew she was about to be discovered. She felt the way she did in the doctor's office when she had all her clothes off and sat waiting for

Dr. Watson to come in and say, "What's wrong with Leona Hanrahan today?"

Leona closed her eyes and braced herself for Mom to scream "Leona!" There was no scream. Leona waited. She heard the door squeak open and bang shut. She opened her eyes.

She saw Victoria carry the cups to the table. Victoria was wearing a sleek new pair of jeans and a baggy pink blouse. Albert followed her with a sack of chips in one hand and a brand-new toy toolbox in the other. He helped himself and stuffed a handful of chips into his mouth. Then he trotted over to the swing and Victoria followed him.

"Up you go, Albert." Victoria heaved him into the higher of the two swings. Then she began to push. He sang a song about his bonny and the ocean. Over and over he sang the same words and Victoria pushed him and laughed. She looked as if she was actually having fun. She didn't act like playing with Albert was a chore at all.

Leona got a funny feeling, like that empty feeling when you don't get invited to a party. It started in her stomach, then made a little chill run up her arms and back. She felt cold even though she was sitting on a hot roof in the sun. And she felt sad.

Mom was talking to Aunt Gwendolyn, laughing and talking. Victoria wore new clothes. Albert had a new toy. They were having a great time together. Everyone was happy. Life went on smoothly without her. No one seemed to care that she was missing.

Leona gripped her purse and made a vow to run away, if she ever got down from the roof.

Leona had no idea that it took grown-ups so long to look up. She cleared her throat, which felt dry and scratchy. She wondered if she would ever be able to talk again. Then she heard the loud rumble and roar of a motor.

Rumble, rumble, vroom, vroom, va-room.

Leona looked up. A red pickup truck was coming down the alley and turned into the back driveway. It was pulling a house trailer, and in the back of the pickup was the biggest, shiniest motorcycle Leona had ever seen. It must be Uncle Rosco.

The trailer was not shiny. It was blue and white with red rust spots all over the sides. When the truck stopped, the trailer stuck out into the alley a little. It had big oval windows like the ones in the boats Leona had seen on Lake Michigan. Leona had always wanted to ride in one of those boats. She couldn't wait to go into Uncle Rosco's trailer. It must be great to live in a house on wheels. It was just the right size for a kid.

Leona squirmed. She wished she could fly. She would glide right down and say, "Hi, Uncle Rosco. I'm Leona. I'm your only relative who can fly." And Uncle Rosco would say, "That's amazing," and he would never forget her.

Uncle Rosco got out of the truck. He was tall and thin and had black hair. He had a dark beard and mustache.

"Hi, everybody." He waved. Then he turned to his motorcycle and checked it over and patted the seat.

"Rosco, what a surprise," said Mom. "We didn't expect you until tomorrow." She ran up to Uncle Rosco and gave him a hug and a kiss.

"Don't you know by now, Mavis, to expect the unexpected from our little brother?" said Aunt Gwendolyn. She hugged Uncle Rosco, too.

"Then you can stay longer," Mom said to Uncle Rosco.

"Sorry, I have to drive to Tulsa day after tomorrow," he said. "That's why I came today."

Victoria and Albert ran up to greet Uncle Rosco. Seeing them so happy and eager made Leona even gloomier.

"So you must be little Albert," Uncle Rosco said. He picked Albert up and swung him around. "Hey, you're not so little," he said, and Albert squealed.

"Do it again," Albert said when Uncle Rosco set him down.

"I'm the oldest," Victoria said.

"Don't tell me," said Uncle Rosco. "Victoria Marie, right?" He bowed and kissed Victoria's hand as if she were a princess.

Then Uncle Rosco glanced up. He looked straight at Leona and smiled. "And who is the kid on the roof?" he said.

10
A House on Wheels

UNCLE ROSCO SET THE LADDER AGAINST THE HOUSE and climbed up to Leona.

"I'm Leona," she said as Uncle Rosco helped her down.

I was right about one thing, Leona thought. Maybe Uncle Rosco doesn't have blond hair and blue eyes, but he is strong. He set her down as if she were a feather. Leona smiled back at him.

Leona expected everyone to be staring at her. They were. Mom and Aunt Gwendolyn and Victoria and Albert. But the way Mom looked at her made Leona feel funny. Mom stared as if Leona were an alien who had just dropped down from a distant galaxy. Mom didn't scold. She didn't say, "Go to your room." She just asked in a tight, high voice. "Why did you sit up there for so long without saying anything, Leona?"

"It's Albert's fault. He threw my purse on the roof. I didn't want to bother you because you were busy. So I got the ladder and climbed up to get it all by myself. I got stuck because Albert knocked the ladder down. I was trying hard to be good. Aunt Gwendolyn said—"

"That's not exactly what I meant," interrupted Aunt Gwendolyn.

"What on earth did you say to the girl, Gwendolyn?" Uncle Rosco said. He tapped Leona on the shoulder. "You don't want to be too good, Leona. People who are too good can just disappear."

That's exactly what Leona had been thinking on the roof.

"I don't think Leona is in any danger of disappearing," said Aunt Gwendolyn.

"She almost did," said Mom. She turned to Albert. "Albert, did you throw Leona's purse on the roof?"

"No," said Albert. "It flew."

"Albert, that was wrong. You must not throw anything on the roof, especially something that does not belong to you. Do you understand?"

Albert nodded his head.

"Now I think we should all sit down and eat lunch," Mom said. "I'll bring you a sandwich, Rosco, and you, too, Leona. You must be hungry."

"I'm mostly thirsty," said Leona. She drank a whole glass of lemonade that Aunt Gwendolyn poured for her.

Daddy came out of his office to say hi to Uncle Rosco and have lunch with them. He was in a good mood because he had finally solved a problem he had been working on for a long time. Leona was glad he was in a good mood. When Mom told him Leona had been stuck on the roof of the fireplace room, he just said, "What an odd place." Then he invited everyone out to dinner at a restaurant to celebrate and to give Mom a break from cooking.

Leona liked Uncle Rosco instantly. He really looked at her, not over the top of her head the way some grown-ups do. When she asked if she could see the inside of his trailer, he didn't say, "Out of the question," "No way," or "Get lost." He said, "Maybe after lunch. I ought to straighten it up a little first."

Leona showed Uncle Rosco her purse after she put her supplies back in it. He was interested. She showed him her baseball cards and toothbrush, but not the piece of blanket or the glass monkey. The monkey belonged to Victoria. She was going to tell him why she kept them in her purse, but she decided to wait until they were all alone. The time was not right. Leona had been on earth long enough to know just how important timing is. She especially knew about bad timing. Jumping off the high dive yesterday had been bad timing. Leona didn't want to mess up the plan that was forming in her mind. She didn't want to say anything too soon.

"Can I sit by you at the restaurant tonight?" Leona asked.

"It's a date," Uncle Rosco said, and headed for his trailer.

Leona ran into the kitchen for more lemonade. She drank six more cups. The lemonade was so cold it made her stomach hurt. Leona started to put the lemonade back in the fridge.

"Wait," Mom said. "I'm going to refill Aunt Gwendolyn's and Victoria's cups."

The pitcher jerked up when Mom took it. "Why Leona, you drank more than a quart of lemonade!"

"Sitting on the roof made me thirsty," Leona said.

Shaking her head, Mom got a can of lemonade from the freezer and set it on the counter.

"Leona," Uncle Rosco called. "I'm going to show you kids my trailer now."

Leona banged the screen door open and ran outside. Albert and Victoria, too? She was disappointed. At least he hadn't forgotten her.

"I haven't done a very good cleaning job," Uncle Rosco apologized. "Just close your eyes in the bathroom and kitchen."

He must be joking, Leona thought. How could she see if she closed her eyes?

Albert scrambled ahead when Uncle Rosco opened the door. Victoria ran after him saying, "Don't touch."

Leona stepped into the living room, which was also a kitchen and dining room. By a window were two chairs and a table. Two steps away was the sink.

"You don't have to go far to carry your dishes to the sink, do you, Uncle Rosco?" Leona said.

The sink was piled with dirty dishes. Unwashed mugs and plates stood on the tiny counter, too. Beneath the counter was a small refrigerator.

"Albert, don't bounce on the sofa," Victoria said.

Albert jumped down and rushed to open a door at the end of the trailer.

Leona raced to see the room, too.

"Guns," said Albert. He pointed to a rack of rifles on the wall. *"Bang. Bang."*

Leona was glad the guns were beyond Albert's reach. She stepped over a stack of motorcycle magazines and looked at the pictures on the wall. All were pictures of Uncle Rosco on his motorcycle, except for one. It was a large photo of a pretty woman, signed "Love, Diane." There were trophies on another shelf and in boxes on the floor.

I could put my sleeping bag on the floor here, Leona thought, after I pick up the boxes.

"Do you live here all alone?" Leona asked.

Uncle Rosco nodded. "I was going to get a cat once. But cats don't like to travel."

"Don't you get lonely?"

"Sometimes. I'm pretty busy most of the time," Uncle Rosco said.

"Where do you sleep?" Leona asked. She peeked into the kid-sized bathroom.

"On the sofa," Uncle Rosco said. "It folds out if I move the table. It must seem cramped to you."

"It is pretty little," Victoria said. "Rita's dad sets up a tent in their backyard in August and it's bigger than this."

"Uncle Rosco's house is beautiful." Leona frowned at Victoria. Then she noticed a tiny television set at the end of the counter next to the toaster. "It's perfect. It's got everything." She clapped her hands together and turned around to show Uncle Rosco how much room there was.

Albert stumbled into Leona. He was carrying a tall trophy.

Uncle Rosco bent down and grabbed the trophy before Albert dropped it. "Whoa, Albert. That's the biggest one I have. You know, I broke my toe the day I won that trophy."

Leona looked at Uncle Rosco's black leather boots. "Which toe?"

Uncle Rosco sat down, tugged at his right boot until it came off, then peeled off his wrinkled sock. He wiggled his toes and pointed to his big toe. "This one."

Leona looked closely. "It doesn't look broken."

"That's because it's healed," Victoria pointed out.

"Did you crash?" said Leona. She thought it would be a miracle to crash and just break your big toe, and not your arms and legs and your head, too.

"No," Uncle Rosco said. "My girlfriend came up to congratulate me. When she kissed me, I dropped the trophy on my toe."

"How romantic," said Victoria.

Leona knew what it was like to hurt yourself in strange accidents. "That's too bad, Uncle Rosco," she said with sincerity. Then she added, "Tell us about the races you won."

Leona, Victoria, and Albert sat in Uncle Rosco's tiny kitchen, and Uncle Rosco talked about motor-

cycle races until it was time to get ready to go to the restaurant.

Leona sat beside Uncle Rosco at the restaurant. She was wearing the dress that Aunt Gwendolyn had bought for her. But she didn't feel elegant. And she didn't feel grateful. It was a dark-blue sailor dress with one pleat in front and one pleat in back and a big square collar and a red scarf that she tied in a knot under the collar. Aunt Gwendolyn wasn't wearing a sailor dress. She looked elegant in a flowered dress and a pearl necklace and earrings.

Leona wanted to ask Uncle Rosco more questions about how lonely he felt. She wanted to find out if he liked kids. He seemed to. But Mom and Dad and Aunt Gwendolyn kept talking to him. Another problem was that Leona had to keep getting up to go to the bathroom.

"All that lemonade," Mom said.

Leona spent more time in the bathroom than at the table.

Then Leona fell asleep in the van on the way home. That's what Mom told her. "Wake up, Leona. We're home."

Leona didn't have much chance to talk to Uncle Rosco at all that evening.

Mom carried Albert inside and Leona stumbled behind her. She was too tired to try to untie the knot in her scarf. She climbed into bed and slid under the sheet with her sailor dress on.

In the middle of the night, Leona woke up to go to the bathroom. Before she got back into bed, she looked out the window at the trailer in the driveway. Uncle Rosco was staying in his trailer because there weren't enough rooms in the house.

A light glowed yellow through the trailer window. It looked warm and cozy.

"It's perfect," Leona whispered. "Just perfect." She wondered what it would be like to live in a house on wheels.

11
Uncle Rosco

WHEN LEONA WOKE AGAIN, IT WAS STILL DARK OUT. She tried to go back to sleep, but she couldn't. She was thinking about Uncle Rosco and his trailer.

Very quietly she climbed out of bed and tiptoed downstairs. No one was up yet. Out the kitchen window, she could see a pale line of light above the treetops. It would be morning soon. She hoped Uncle Rosco liked to get up early. She sneaked out the kitchen door.

Leona stood on the trailer steps ready to knock on Uncle Rosco's door. But it was dark and quiet inside. She sat down on the top step. Huddling against the door, she waited. She yawned. Her eyelids got heavy and she tried to hold them open.

"Well, if it isn't Leona the roofsitter. Come on in and have a cup of coffee."

Leona blinked. The sun was shining. She sat up straight and rubbed her eyes. "Hi, Uncle Rosco. You're finally awake."

"And so are you," said Uncle Rosco. "Like I said, come on in."

Leona sat down at the table. Uncle Rosco rescued two mugs from the pile by the sink. He rinsed them out and set them on the table. He filled one mug with hot coffee. He dribbled a little coffee in the other and then poured in milk. He stirred in two small packets of sugar with a popsicle stick and set the mug in front of Leona.

Leona had never drunk coffee before. Mom said it wasn't good for kids. But if she was going to live with Uncle Rosco, he would probably expect her to drink it.

"You're real dressed up this morning, Leona. Did you just drop in for an early morning visit, or can I do something for you?"

Leona smoothed her wrinkled sailor dress. She wished she had something else on, but she couldn't get the knot untied. She wasn't going to ask Uncle Rosco to help. He would think she was a baby.

"I have a question to ask," Leona said. "Where's Tulsa, Uncle Rosco?"

"It's in Oklahoma. Tulsa is pretty far away from Winnetka. I hope you didn't stay up all night thinking about Tulsa."

Leona felt her cheeks get warm. "I was just wondering, Uncle Rosco." Leona tried to sip her coffee very casually. "Are you going to miss me when you leave?" The coffee was good. It tasted like melted coffee ice cream.

"Of course I will," said Uncle Rosco. "When you're busy and traveling all the time, you still get tired of being alone. I'm glad I came to see you. It's nice to be with family."

That depends on the family, Leona thought. "You like kids, don't you, Uncle Rosco? Did you ever want kids of your own?"

"I never really thought about it. Yeah, kids are okay, especially when they don't get in the way." He winked and Leona thought he might be joking. Or maybe he was talking about Albert. Albert was always in the way. Uncle Rosco had probably already noticed.

"I'm very good at staying out of the way," Leona said. "I'm helpful, too." Leona thought about the chores she did at home. Loading the dishwasher. Picking up her room. Helping Mom fold the laundry. She didn't like to fold laundry or to pick up her room, but she could learn to like doing it if she had to. "I think you need someone to do the dishes."

"Not a bad idea, Leona," Uncle Rosco said.

"I know who could do the dishes for you."

"Who?" Uncle Rosco seemed interested.

"Me," Leona said.

"Thanks, Leona. That's nice of you. But we're going on a family picnic today. I would hate to put you to work."

"How about tomorrow?"

"We'll see. But I have to leave tomorrow. Going to Tulsa."

"I know," said Leona. "Maybe I could travel with you."

"Do you like to travel?" Uncle Rosco asked. His dark-brown eyes sparkled like the coffee in his mug.

Leona didn't answer right away. She was too

surprised. Instead of saying no, Uncle Rosco was prac-
tically inviting her to go along. Leona thought about
the vacation her family took once. They went all the
way to Washington, D.C.—Mom and Dad and Leona
and Victoria. Albert wasn't around yet. "That's where
Albert started," Mom and Dad always said. Leona
thought it was kind of silly to drive all the way to
Washington, D.C., to start someone like Albert.

Leona had traveled to Chicago, too. It wasn't
far, but she went on the train with Mom and Victoria.

"I just love to travel," Leona said. "I want to go
around the world someday."

"I don't go quite that far," said Uncle Rosco.
"But I am on the road a lot. I never seem to stay in
one place long. You know, I don't get back to the
Chicago area very often, either."

"That's all right," said Leona. "Mom and Daddy
wouldn't miss me."

Uncle Rosco raised one dark eyebrow. He didn't
believe her. He had probably never heard of parents
who didn't pay attention to someone like Leona. She
would have to convince him.

"Mom and Daddy have Victoria and Albert,"
Leona said. "Dad is busy most of the time with his
computers, but when he isn't, he does things with
Victoria, things that I can't do because I'm not old
enough. And Albert is always hanging on Mom. I
don't see how she can stand it."

"Leona, I'm sure they care very much about you,
too."

"You haven't been here long enough," Leona said. "You should have seen what Mom did when I fell off Rita's ten-speed and scraped my knee. She said, 'I can't put a big Band-Aid on your knee.' She didn't, either. And that was a big owie." Leona showed Uncle Rosco her scraped knee and he winced.

"Then I jumped off the high board, which is really something for a little kid like me. All Mom could do was yell at me for taking a long shower. Victoria had makeup on and when I put a little on, I got in trouble. You saw how I got stuck on the roof because of Albert. If you hadn't come, I would probably still be up there." Talking about it all again made Leona feel sorry for herself.

"Sounds like a rough week," said Uncle Rosco.

"It's always like that," said Leona.

"Maybe you need a vacation."

"To Tulsa," Leona said.

Uncle Rosco laughed and raised his mug. "To Tulsa," he said and clinked his mug against Leona's.

And wasn't that the same as saying "Yes, Leona, you can come and live with me"?

12
Motorcycles Are Better Than Ten-Speeds

LEONA WANTED TO SPEND THE WHOLE MORNING with Uncle Rosco. She had so many things to talk about. But Mom came to the trailer and told Uncle Rosco everyone was having brunch. Mom told Leona to change her clothes.

"I'll see you at brunch, Uncle Rosco." Leona ran back to the house and went upstairs to her room. Victoria had put on her new jeans and pink blouse. She was brushing her hair and staring at herself in the dresser mirror.

"Could you help me?" Leona pulled at the scarf knotted around her neck.

Victoria put her brush down and helped Leona untie the scarf. "Leona, you slept in your new dress! Look how wrinkled it is."

"It doesn't matter," Leona said. "I'm not wearing it today." She thought, I'll never wear it again. Uncle Rosco will let me wear what I want to. She put her bathing suit on under her flowered green skirt and white T-shirt with the lace collar.

"You don't have to put your suit on yet. We're not going to Lake Michigan until this afternoon."

"I want to be ready," Leona said. She hugged her lavender purse to her heart. "Ready for anything."

"Don't be so dramatic," Victoria said.

If Victoria knew what was happening tomorrow, she would be dramatic, too. Leona thought maybe she should tell Victoria. After all, Victoria was her only sister. No, she decided, then Victoria would want to come along, too.

After brunch Mom, Aunt Gwendolyn, and Uncle Rosco sat around drinking coffee. Even Daddy stayed with them.

Leona asked for coffee, but Mom said, "No, Leona, coffee is bad for you."

Uncle Rosco looked at Leona and put his fingers to his lips, so Leona didn't say she had already drunk some coffee. But she wondered why grown-ups drank so much coffee if it was that bad for you.

Daddy was the first to get up. "Excuse me, everyone. I just have to do a few things in my office before the picnic."

"And I have to get my motorcycle down if I'm going to ride it today," said Uncle Rosco.

Albert headed for the back door. Leona leaped after him, pushed him out of the way, and ran out to the truck.

"Uncle Rosco, can you take me for a ride on your motorcycle?" she shouted as Uncle Rosco came out the door. She felt a little nervous that he might say yes. But she had to ask before Albert did. She knew that's what Albert was up to. She shouldn't have shoved Albert, but she wanted to be first on the motorcycle. She couldn't always be good and kind and thoughtful and helpful. Hadn't Uncle Rosco said yesterday that a person could be too good? Besides, if she was going to live with a motorcycle racer, she ought to find out what it was like to ride a motorcycle.

"I think we should take turns," Victoria said, following Uncle Rosco and Albert. "I'm the oldest, so I should go first."

"I'm the youngest," said Albert. "Me first."

"Albert, you are too young," Mom shouted from the back door.

"Tell you what," said Uncle Rosco.

Leona crossed her fingers.

"I'll take the one in the middle first. When we go to the lake, I'll take Leona. Albert can sit on my bike when I park it at the beach, and Victoria can have a ride back with me."

"Yippee! Yippee! Yay!" Leona yelled. She knew she could count on Uncle Rosco.

Leona held on tight to Uncle Rosco.

Brumble, brumble, broom, broom, broom. The engine started and they took off.

It was kind of like flying. They passed bushes and fences and trees with no effort. Leona saw Rita at the corner, but she didn't dare let go of Uncle Rosco to wave. She wanted to tell Rita motorcycles are better than ten-speeds. You don't have to pedal.

Motorcycles are like roller coasters, too, Leona thought as they bumped across the railroad track. Her stomach began to feel funny.

Houses flew by; so did the stores on Linden Avenue. Then more houses and a park and the fence along the highway. Leona was dizzy when they arrived at the lake. She jumped off by herself. The ground was shaking. Maybe Leona was shaking. Everything was quiet when Uncle Rosco shut off the engine, except her ears kept ringing.

"How was the ride?" Uncle Rosco said.

"Great," Leona said, hearing her voice rattle.

"You should feel what it's like to race one, to go a hundred and twenty miles per hour with the wind whizzing past. Super!" Uncle Rosco put the helmets in the saddlebags.

Leona figured that going 120 with the wind whizzing past might take a while to get used to.

"Let's get our feet wet." Uncle Rosco trotted toward the beach. He sat down in the sand and took his boots and socks off. Then he ran straight into the water, without even rolling his jeans up.

Leona laughed. That was the most wonderful thing she had ever seen anyone do. She slipped off her sandals and headed for the water. Together they splashed along the beach, teasing the waves. Uncle Rosco swooped her up and set her on his shoulders. He waded out deeper and Leona could feel the cold wave spray in her face.

"I don't want the waves to ever stop," Leona said.

"They won't," said Uncle Rosco. He walked out of the water and set Leona onto the dry sand.

"My turn. My turn. I want a piggyback ride."

It was Albert. The others had arrived. Albert ran toward Leona and Uncle Rosco. Then he tripped and did a belly flop right at Uncle Rosco's feet.

Leona should have been mad. Albert was butting in again. But instead, she laughed. Albert looked so funny. Besides, she was going to have Uncle Rosco all to herself tomorrow.

Leona bent down and helped Albert up. "Are you okay, Albert?" She wondered what it would be like not to have Albert around.

"I'm okay," said Albert. He brushed sand off his legs and arms.

That was one good thing about Albert. He almost never cried, even when it hurt.

Uncle Rosco put Albert on his shoulders and they walked up to the others. Mom and Aunt Gwendolyn had spread a quilt in the shade at the edge of the park where the beach began. They decided to have something to drink and some chips. Then they would go for a little walk on the pier before they did what Daddy called "serious eating."

They all sat down together on the quilt, except Albert. He sat on Uncle Rosco's motorcycle and refused to move.

As they ate, the grown-ups started talking about when they were kids.

"Do you remember that time you tried to run away, Mavis?" Uncle Rosco said to Mom.

Leona stopped crunching her chips and stared at Mom.

Mom laughed. "Yes, I do. I was mad at Mother

and Dad, and when I asked Gwendolyn what to do, she told me to run away. Gwendolyn, you even helped me pack my bag."

"Oh, Mavis, I didn't." Aunt Gwendolyn laughed.

"Did you really run away, Mom?" said Leona. Who did Mom go to live with? Didn't she miss her mom and daddy?

"Yes," Mom said. "I spent the whole afternoon with Mrs. Jackson, who lived two blocks away. But I forgot my toothbrush, so I went back home."

Everyone laughed, but Leona. Leona opened her purse to check if her toothbrush was there. It was. Then she picked up the glass monkey. He looked like he was laughing, too. Leona had never noticed how silly his grin was. Maybe she should give him back to Victoria. Even if Victoria didn't play with him anymore, he still belonged to her.

If Leona took the monkey to Tulsa, it would be far away. Leona nudged Victoria and showed her the monkey. "Do you want your monkey back?"

Victoria smiled. "No, you keep it," she said.

Why is she being so nice to me? Leona wondered. She doesn't even know that I am leaving tomorrow. She doesn't know that I am taking her glass monkey far away.

But Leona knew. She put the monkey back in her purse. Leona had the feeling that being far away was not the same as being home.

13
Leona in the Water

"DADDY, LET'S GO OUT ON THE PIER NOW AND show Aunt Gwendolyn and Uncle Rosco the sailboats," Victoria said.

Daddy stood up and rubbed his hands together. "All right, everyone. Onward." He pointed to the pier.

"Do you think we should leave everything here?" Mom said.

"Sure. It will be fine," said Daddy. "We aren't going far."

Leona looked up. She had been rearranging her baseball cards. "Well, I'm taking my purse," she said. "Somebody might steal it."

By the time she put her cards in order and slipped a rubber band around them, the others were way ahead. Daddy, Aunt Gwendolyn, and Victoria first. Then Mom, Uncle Rosco, and Albert.

The pier stretched above the water far out into the lake. There was a fisherman sitting on the edge and there was a woman with curly white hair painting a picture.

Leona ran to catch up. She could hear Victoria talking.

"That's a tackle box." Victoria pointed to a box beside the fisherman.

The fisherman chuckled and asked, "Do you know what's in it?"

"Of course," said Victoria. "Hooks and sinkers and lures."

"Been fishing before?" said the fisherman.

Daddy put his hand on Victoria's shoulder. "She's a fine fisherman," he said.

Aunt Gwendolyn nodded approvingly.

"So am I. So am I," Leona chanted to herself. "I can catch fish, too." Then she thought, What do I care? Uncle Rosco will find out how good I am at fishing. But Leona did care. She wanted Daddy to tell a complete stranger that she was a good fisherman, too.

From Uncle Rosco's shoulders Albert pointed at the woman's painting. "Blue," he said. "Blue for sky. Blue for lake."

"What an adorable child," said the painter.

Mom reached up and patted Albert's face. "He's my youngest."

"So what," Leona murmured.

Hooks and sinkers and lures aren't the only things in tackle boxes, Leona said to herself. There's a stringer for fish you catch, and extra line, in case you get a snag, and a pocketknife. Everyone knows that. I know all the colors, too, not just blue.

"Red, orange, yellow, green, blue, indigo, violet!" Leona shouted.

No one in her family heard her. They were walking toward the end of the pier. The painter nodded at Leona and went back to her painting. The fisherman stared at the lake.

There they go again, Leona thought. Why is it so easy to forget about me? Is it because I'm in the middle? But I don't want everyone to forget about me. They act as if I'm not here. Well, I won't be here if I go with Uncle Rosco tomorrow. But then they will forget all about me forever. I won't even be around to get yelled at.

Leona didn't like to be yelled at, but at least when someone yelled at her, she was being noticed. She knew she was there.

Uncle Rosco looked over his shoulder at Leona and winked.

Leona tried to smile, but she couldn't. She felt mixed-up inside. She had been planning to run away for a long time. She finally had found a place to go to. Tomorrow she would travel to Tulsa with Uncle Rosco. Tomorrow she would leave her family, but suddenly she didn't know if she wanted to leave or not.

If only Mom or Daddy or Victoria or even Albert would turn around and say, "Don't go, Leona. We couldn't live without you," then she would stay. If someone would make a sign, a small sign—Leona would stay.

But Albert was holding Uncle Rosco's hand and singing, "My bonny, my bonny, my ocean." He pulled Uncle Rosco to move faster. Victoria was at

the end of the pier with Daddy and Aunt Gwendolyn.
Victoria pointed to the sailboats. Daddy and Aunt
Gwendolyn looked out at the lake with their hands
cupped over their eyes. They didn't even notice that
Leona wasn't with them. Would they notice she was
gone tomorrow? Would they miss her?

Leona squeezed her purse and bit her lower lip.
She tried to make a picture in her mind of Uncle
Rosco's cozy trailer and the mugful of coffee and milk,
but she kept seeing the kitchen table in her own
house. Everyone was sitting around it: Mom, Daddy,
Victoria, Albert, and Leona herself. She was eating
and laughing and talking with the whole family.

Leona blinked and shook her head. She stared
down at the lake. She couldn't see the bottom. It was
deep. Suddenly, a little wild duck swam around a
column under the pier and paddled to a spot right in
front of her.

"What are you doing here all alone?" Leona said
to the duck.

The little duck swam in circles. It looked hungry. Leona took the cracker package from her purse.
She crumbled up the crackers, unwrapped the package, and tossed the pieces to the duck.

The duck quacked, then jabbed his bill at the
crackers floating on the surface of the lake. Suddenly,
a whole flock of little ducklings swam up. The plump
mother duck skimmed over to the crackers and helped
herself to a few soggy crumbs.

"Here, little duck." Leona felt sorry for the
duck. She wanted him to get his fair share of crumbs.

"Quick, get these crumbs." Leona clenched the last crumbs in her fist. She raised her hand as if she was going to throw a baseball, fast and hard. She cocked her arm back, then whizzed it forward. She followed through on the pitch, lost her balance, and fell into Lake Michigan.

The chill of the water took Leona's breath away for a moment. Duck and ducklings scattered. Crumbs scattered. Holding tight to her purse, Leona began to kick. She held her head up high out of the water.

"Man overboard! Someone's fallen overboard," the fisherman shouted.

"It's Leona. Leona's in the water," Victoria cried out and ran back down the pier.

The whole family followed. Soon everyone stood on the pier above Leona. Albert pointed and yelled, "Leona. Ocean." Uncle Rosco took off his boots. Mom lay flat on the pier and stretched her arm out. The fisherman handed Daddy a pole. Daddy held the fat end toward Leona. She clung to the pole and Daddy pulled her to the pier. When Mom could reach her, she clutched Leona by the shoulder. Uncle Rosco held her other shoulder. Together, Mom and Daddy and Uncle Rosco pulled Leona onto the pier.

Leona sat there for a minute, dripping, wondering how she had gotten from just standing on the pier, looking at the lake, to actually being in the water. Everything had happened so fast. She held up her soggy purse to show that she had saved it, too.

Mom was silent. Her stare went from the purse

to Leona. On her face was that strange look she had had when Leona had come down from the roof. It was more than a look. It was a seeing look.

Mom put her arms around Leona and hugged her dripping and all. Daddy knelt beside them and hugged both Mom and Leona.

"Leona, Leona, Leona," Mom kept saying. She crunched Leona so tight she couldn't breathe.

Leona started to explain.

"No, you don't have to say anything," said Mom. "But oh, that was a scare."

"You did the right thing," said Daddy. "You didn't panic."

"You're a very good swimmer," said Uncle Rosco.

"And you didn't even lose your purse," said Aunt Gwendolyn.

"Wow, Leona," Victoria said. "You could have drowned." She stared at Leona with her mouth open, and Albert repeated, "Leona, ocean. Leona, ocean."

14
Leona in the Middle

WRAPPED IN A BEACH TOWEL, LEONA SAT BETWEEN Mom and Daddy on the quilt while they all ate their picnic supper. Never had a ham loaf sandwich tasted so good. Leona even ate a deviled egg and liked it although she knew it had mayonnaise in it.

When she finished, she didn't want to move.

"Do you feel all right?" Mom asked.

"Yes," said Leona.

"Maybe you would rather go home and rest," Daddy said.

"Oh, no," said Leona. "I just want to sit here and listen to grown-up talk for a while."

"Are you sure you're all right?" Mom said.

"Um-hm." Leona nodded. Even if the grown-up talk got boring, Leona wanted to stay. She wanted to stay in the middle between Mom and Daddy, where she felt warm and safe and happy.

"Don't you want to come down to the beach?" Victoria said. "I'm going to make a sand castle with Albert. I'll race you."

But Leona didn't feel like racing Victoria to the beach, and she didn't want to make a bigger, better sand castle than Albert.

"Not now," Leona said. "Maybe later."

"Okay." Victoria shrugged and ran toward the lake with Albert.

Uncle Rosco filled a plastic cup with coffee from a thermos and sat down on the quilt. "Do you know who Leona reminds me of?" he said, smiling at Leona.

"Who?" said Mom.

Uncle Rosco laughed and pointed at Mom. "You."

Mom squeezed Leona by the shoulders. "I suppose so," she murmured. "My hair used to be blond, too, but it got darker."

"You were very accident-prone," Aunt Gwendolyn said. "Remember when you mashed your thumb in the car door on vacation and we had to drive for hours to find a hospital?"

"That really hurt," said Mom.

Leona took Mom's hands and looked at both thumbs. "They look okay now."

"That was a long time ago," said Mom, holding up her right thumb.

"Like the cowboy boots," said Leona. Suddenly, she had a picture in her mind of Mom in a cowboy outfit. Mom was holding her thumb and crying. Leona wanted to make Mom feel better, not grown-up Mom, but Mom when she was a little girl. A little girl like Leona. Leona held Mom's right hand and squeezed. Mom squeezed back.

Aunt Gwendolyn was still talking. "And Rosco had to go to the bathroom so bad he turned green. He was afraid to go in the woods."

Everyone but Rosco laughed.

"I know another way I am like Mom," said
Leona. "Only I didn't forget my toothbrush."

"What do you mean?" Mom asked.

"You forgot your toothbrush when you ran
away, Mom."

"But you didn't run away, Leona," Daddy said.
"You fell in the lake."

"But I was going to run away," Leona said.

"Leona?" Mom said softly with a worried look
on her face.

Uncle Rosco cleared his throat. "Let's go see
what Victoria and Albert are up to," he said to Aunt
Gwendolyn.

"All right," said Aunt Gwendolyn. She slipped
her sandals off and strolled toward the lake with Uncle
Rosco.

Leona looked around at the dry beach sand.
There were little pockets of shadows all over the
beach. They seemed to change, to get darker or
lighter. They were like moving ponds of darkness,
never staying in one place.

"Why did you want to run away, Leona?" Daddy
asked.

"Not exactly run away. I was going to live with
Uncle Rosco. We were talking about how much I like
to travel, and he sort of invited me to go to Tulsa."

"To Tulsa?" said Mom. "But why did you want
to leave?"

"Because." Leona thought for a moment. "I like
him. I like his house on wheels. And he doesn't have
any kids. He's not even married, so he must be lonely.

And I didn't think you would miss me." That was
the truth. That's exactly what Leona had thought,
but when she said the words out loud, she didn't
believe them anymore.

"Why?" Mom repeated.

Then it all came out. The things Leona thought,
the things she felt, the things she didn't believe anymore. She felt like she was racing downhill on a ten-
speed and couldn't stop.

"You always pay attention to Victoria. She's the
oldest. She's the smartest. She has the most talent.
She gets to do everything first. She gets to have everything first. She even gets to wear glasses. And Albert
is cute and cuddly to you. You act like he is a teddy
bear. You never get mad at Albert and sometimes he
can be a real brat. It's like maybe you love them more
than you do me. Sometimes I feel like I don't fit in."

Leona stopped suddenly. Everything was quiet.
The shadows on the beach had gotten longer.

"Leona, I think I see what you mean," said
Daddy. "It's not easy being in the middle. Sometimes
you have to be the strongest."

"I am strong," said Leona, not quite sure what
Daddy meant.

"Are you strong enough to put up with things
that aren't always the way you want them to be?
Strong enough to put up with a little brother and a
big sister? Are you strong enough to tell us when
you're unhappy?"

"Yes, Leona," Mom said. "You should always
tell us about your feelings."

"Oh, that kind of strong," said Leona. She grabbed Mom's arm and Daddy's arm and held tight. "Yes I am. I want to put up with you.

"But what will I tell Uncle Rosco?" she said. "I don't want to hurt his feelings. Can you tell him?"

"I think you should," said Daddy.

"I'm sure he'll understand," said Mom. She bent over and kissed Leona on the head. "I am beginning to understand a lot myself. I'm glad you told us."

"I am, too," said Daddy.

"Me, too," said Leona. "But talking is harder than jumping off the high board."

"You have to be brave to say what you think," said Daddy.

"Leona's our bravest," Mom said.

Leona stood up and stretched. She felt stiff all over from sitting still for so long. She had a great urge to run. "I feel like playing now," she said.

Then she sprinted across the sand, tripping twice, and joined Victoria and Albert. Together they built a giant sand castle. Uncle Rosco helped them fill the moat with lake water and Aunt Gwendolyn got wet sand all over her pastel shorts.

"Never mind," she said. "I'm having fun."

Later, they made a small fire for toasting marshmallows. Leona toasted a marshmallow golden brown and offered it to Uncle Rosco. "Uncle Rosco, you won't be mad at me if I don't go to Tulsa with you, will you?"

Uncle Rosco juggled the hot marshmallow with his fingertips. Then he held it and blew on it for a minute. He didn't look mad. He didn't look as if he was going to cry. He looked as if he was thinking.

Uncle Rosco plopped the whole marshmallow into his mouth, paused a moment, and swallowed it. Then he rubbed his hands together and finally spoke. "How can I ever be mad at anyone who toasts marshmallows like that?"

Leona laughed and toasted him another marshmallow.

"But when I'm older, can I come visit?" she said.

"Of course," said Uncle Rosco. "You come see me. Wherever I am."